D0194998

The
Twelve Days
of
Christmas

[Correspondence]

First published in hardback in 1998 by Doubleday,
a division of Transworld Publishers Ltd.

This edition published in Great Britain in hardback in 2010 by
Atlantic Books, an imprint of Atlantic Books Ltd.

10 9 8 7 6 5 4 3 2 1

A CIP catalogue record for this book is available from the British Library.

Hardback ISBN: 978 1 84887 708 5

Printed in Malta on behalf of Latitude Press

Atlantic Books
An imprint of Atlantic Books Ltd
Ormond House
26 27 Boswell Street
London WC1N 3JZ
www.atlantic-books.co.uk

John Julius Norwich

~

The
TWELVE DAYS
of
CHRISTMAS
[Correspondence]

~

illustrated by
Quentin Blake

Atlantic Books
LONDON

25th December

My dearest darling – That partridge, in that
lovely little pear tree! What an enchanting,
romantic, poetic present! Bless you and thank you.

Your deeply loving Emily

26th December

My dearest darling Edward – The two turtle doves arrived this morning and are cooing away in the pear tree as I write. I'm so touched and grateful.

With undying love, as always, Emily.

27th December

My darling Edward – You do think of the most original presents; whoever thought of sending anybody three French hens? Do they really come all the way from France? It's a pity that we have no chicken coops, but I expect we'll find some. Thank you, anyway, they're heaven.

Your loving Emily

28th December

Dearest Edward – What a surprise – four calling birds arrived this morning. They are very sweet, even if they do call rather loudly – they make telephoning impossible. But I expect they'll calm down when they get used to their new home. Anyway, I'm very grateful – of course I am.

Love from Emily

29th December

$\mathcal{D}$earest Edward – The postman has just delivered
five most beautiful gold rings, one for each finger,
and all fitting perfectly. A really lovely present –
lovelier in a way than birds, which do take rather a
lot of looking after. The four that arrived yesterday
are still making a terrible row, and I'm afraid none of
us got much sleep last night. Mummy says she wants
to use the rings to 'wring' their necks – she's only
joking, I think; though I know what she means.
But I *love* the rings. Bless you.

Love, Emily

30th December

*D*ear Edward – Whatever I expected to find
when I opened the front door this morning,
it certainly wasn't six socking great geese laying
eggs all over the doorstep. Frankly, I rather hoped
you had stopped sending me birds – we have no
room for them and they have already ruined
the croquet lawn. I know you meant well, but –
let's call a halt, shall we?

Love, Emily

31st December

Edward – I thought I said no more birds; but this morning I woke up to find no less than seven swans all trying to get into our tiny goldfish pond. I'd rather not think what happened to the goldfish. The whole house seems to be full of birds – to say nothing of what they leave behind them. Please, please STOP.

Your Emily

Frankly, I think I prefer birds. What am I to do with eight milkmaids – AND their cows? Is this some kind of joke? If so, I'm afraid I don't find it very amusing.

Emily

2nd January

Look here, Edward, this has gone far enough. You say you're sending me nine ladies dancing; all I can say is that judging from the way they dance, they're certainly not ladies. The village just isn't accustomed to seeing a regiment of shameless hussies with nothing on but their lipstick cavorting round the green – and it's Mummy and I who get blamed. If you value our friendship – which I do less and less – kindly stop this ridiculous behaviour at once.

Emily

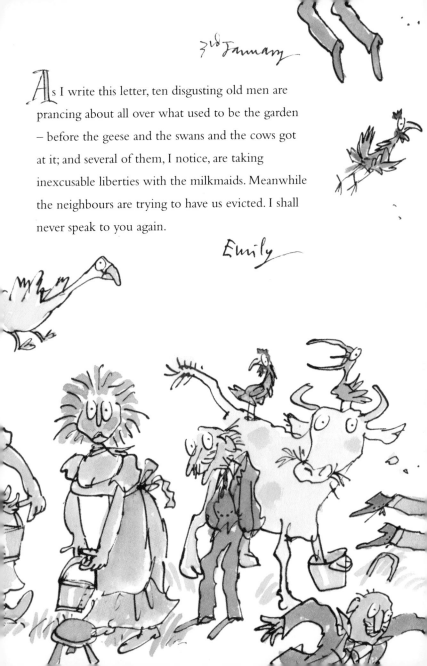

3rd January

As I write this letter, ten disgusting old men are prancing about all over what used to be the garden – before the geese and the swans and the cows got at it; and several of them, I notice, are taking inexcusable liberties with the milkmaids. Meanwhile the neighbours are trying to have us evicted. I shall never speak to you again.

Emily

This is the last straw. You know I detest bagpipes.
The place has now become something between
a menagerie and a madhouse and a man from the
Council has just declared it unfit for habitation.
At least Mummy has been spared this last outrage;
they took her away this afternoon in an ambulance.
I hope you're satisfied.

5th January

Sir,

Our Client, Miss Emily Wilbraham, instructs me to inform you that with the arrival on her premises at half-past seven this morning of the entire percussion section of the Royal Liverpool Philharmonic Orchestra and several of their friends she has no course left open to her but to seek an injunction to prevent your importuning her further.

I am, sir, Yours faithfully,

G. CREEP,
Solicitor-at-Law